# The voyage of PRINCE FUJI

**JENNY THORNE**

Long ago and in a far country lived a man named Fuji who held the rank of Prince.

This book is about a journey he made which turned out to be much longer and much stranger than he expected.

**M**

**For Nicola**

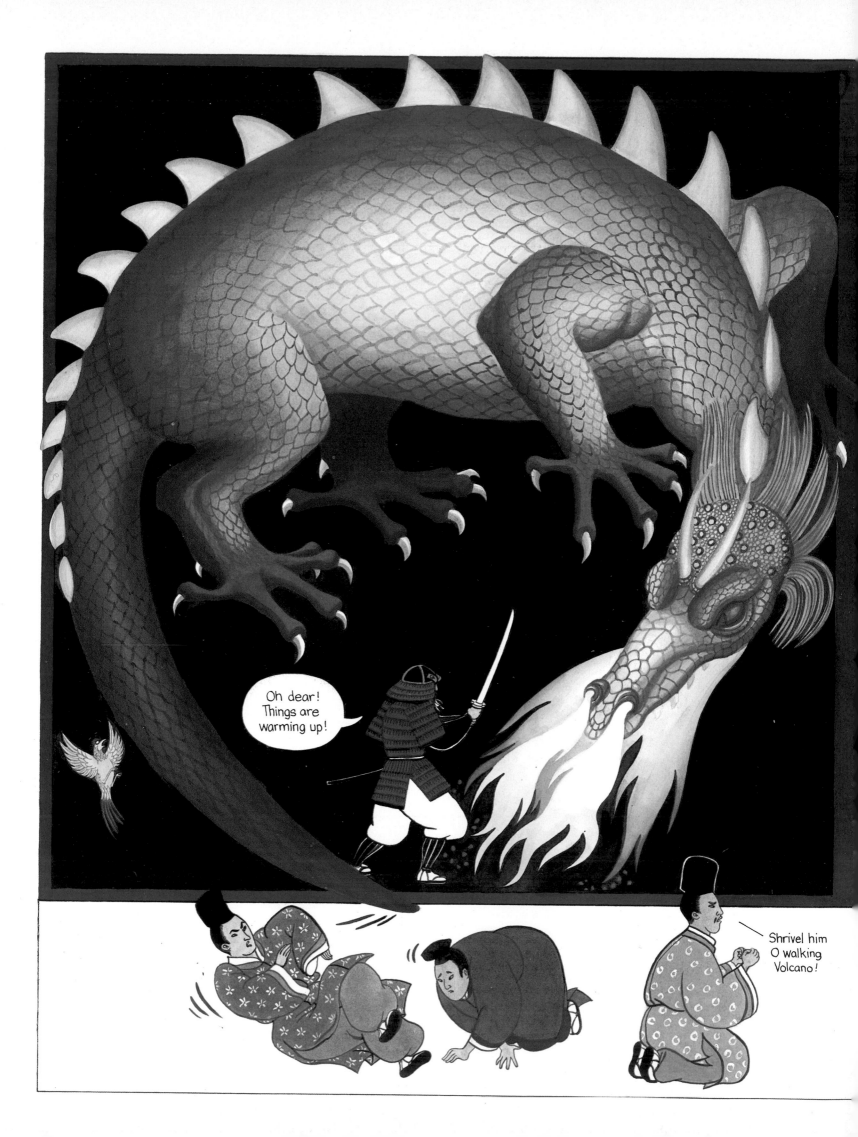

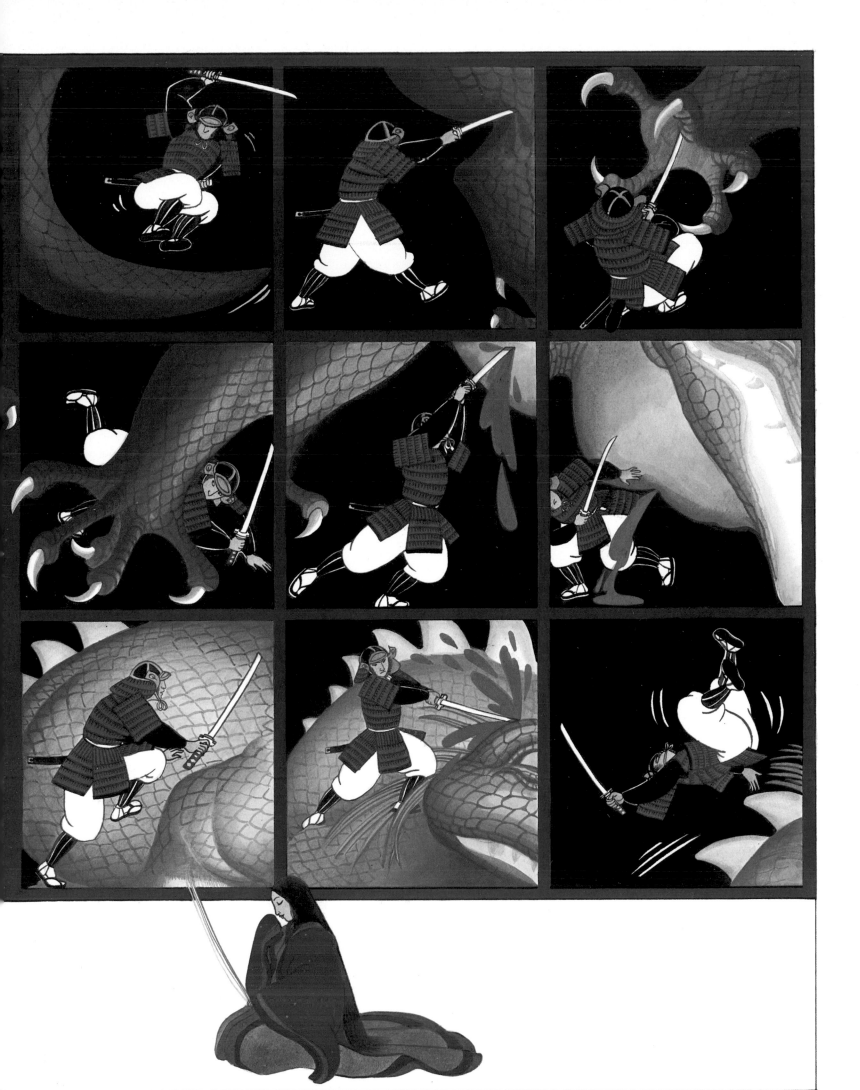

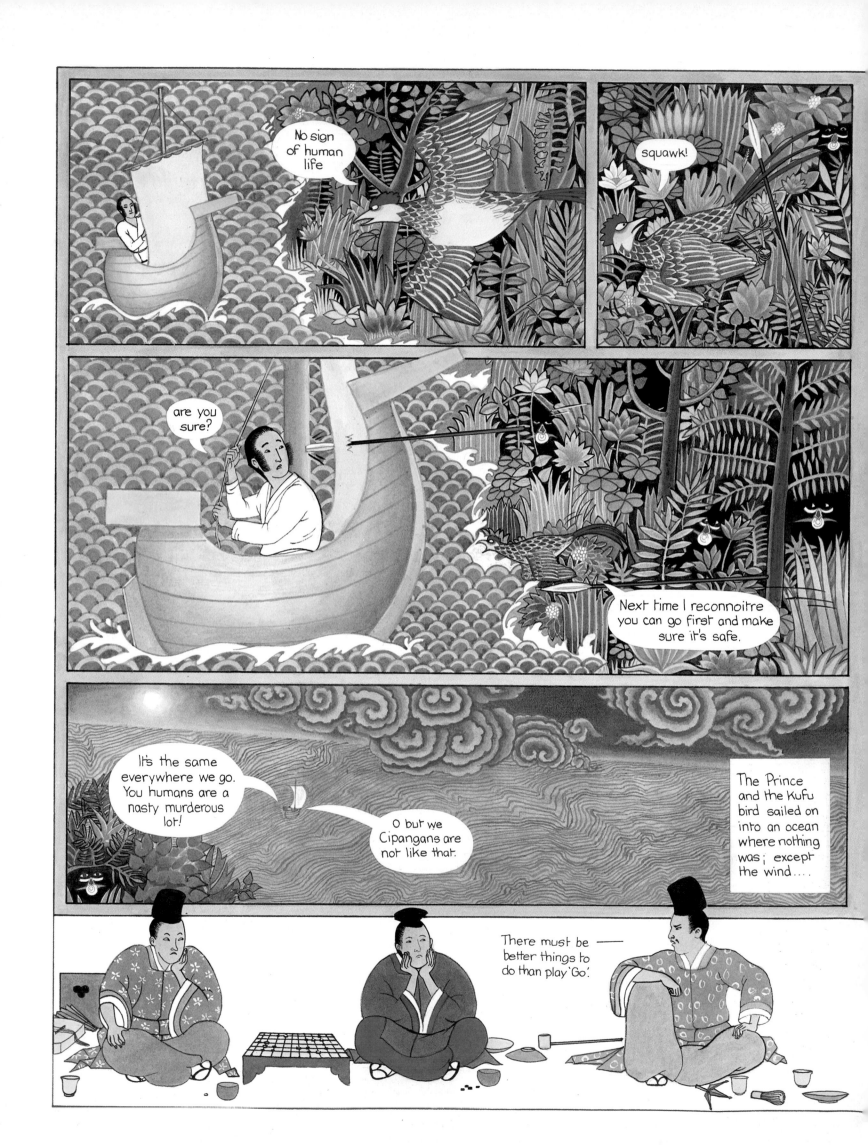

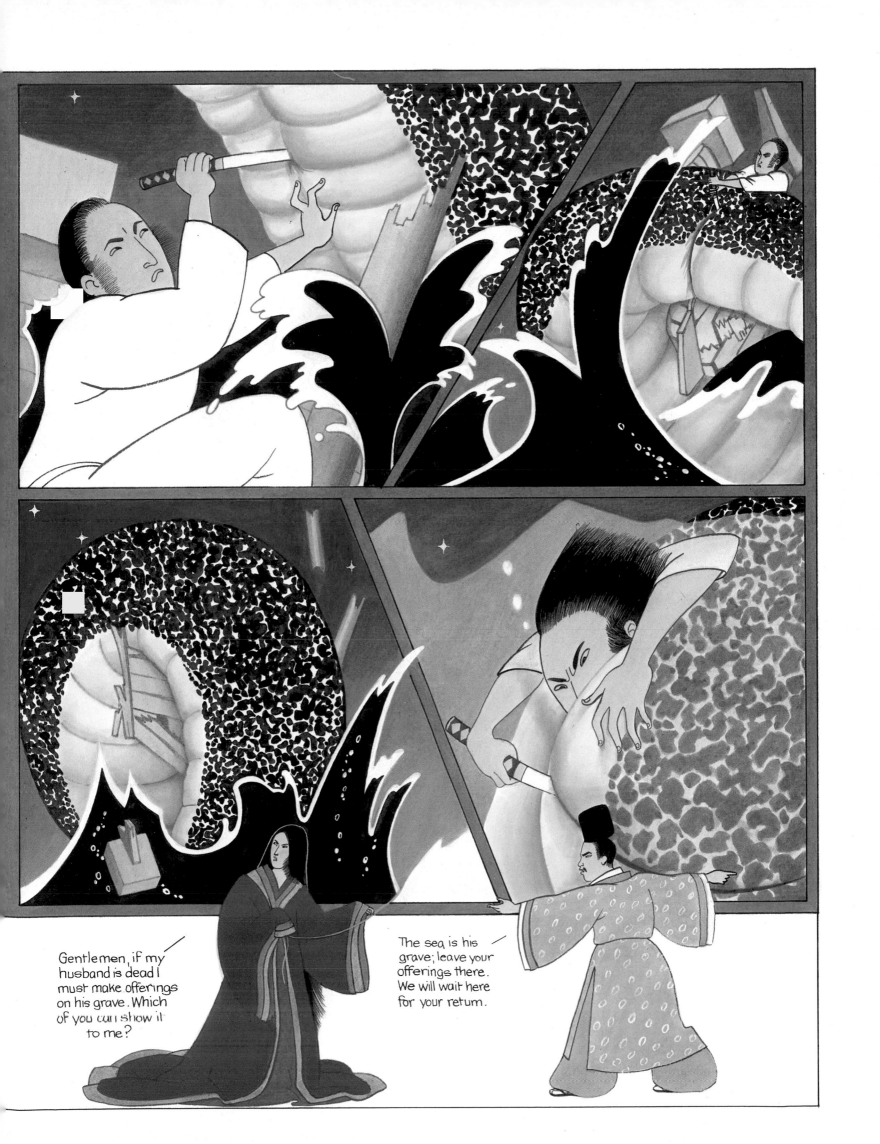

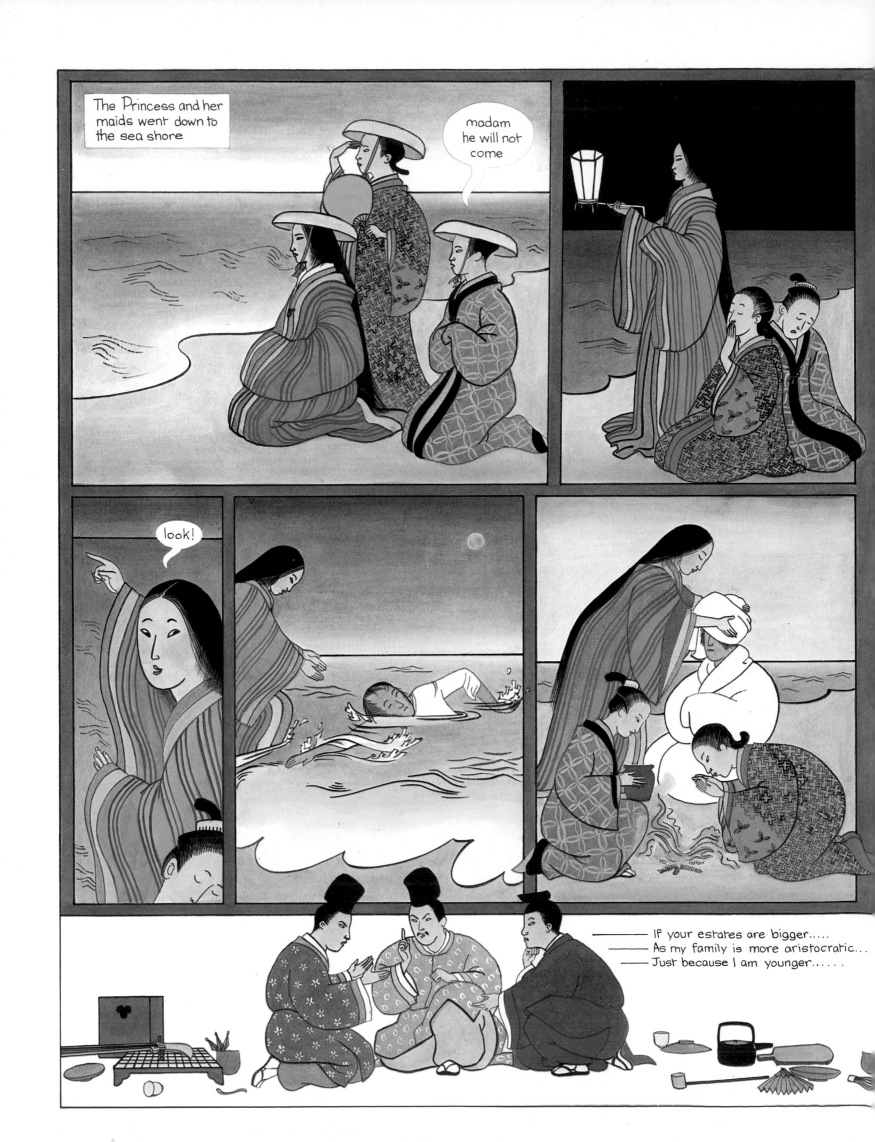

There was still one thing lacking to Prince Fuji's happiness...

Ah! There you are!

The kufu bird!

Prince Fuji settled back into ordinary life; and if at times he looked wistful, it is well known that danger, once passed, possesses an irresistible glamour, and safety, so much prized, is undeniably boring.

My tapestry is finished, I can put away my work box, but for how long? Unfortunately men are not like pet dogs, they cannot be kept on a leash!

©Jenny Thorne 1980

ISBN 0 333 29003 8

*First published 1980 by*
MACMILLAN CHILDREN'S BOOKS
a division of Macmillan Publishers Limited
*4 Little Essex Street London WC2R 3LF*
*and Basingstoke*
*Associated Companies in Delhi, Dublin,*
*Hong Kong, Johannesburg, Lagos, Melbourne,*
*New York, Singapore and Tokyo*

*Printed in Italy*